The King's Taster

For Julia
—Ken

To Michael,
our Top Dog on TKT
—Steve and Lou

The King's Taster
Text copyright © 2009 by Firewing Productions, Inc.
Illustrations copyright © 2009 by Steve Johnson and Lou Fancher

Library of Congress Cataloging-in-Publication Data
Oppel, Kenneth, date
   The king's taster / by Kenneth Oppel ; paintings by Steve Johnson and Lou Fancher. — 1st ed.
      p.   cm.
   Summary: The royal chef takes Max the dog, the royal taster, on several international journeys to find
a dish for the land's pickiest king.
   ISBN 978-0-00-200700-9 (Canada. bdg.)
   [1. Dogs—Fiction. 2. Kings, queen, rulers, etc.—Fiction. 3. Food habits—Fiction. 4. Diet—
Fiction.] I. Johnson, Steve, date, ill. II. Fancher, Lou, ill.
PZ7.O614Ki 2008   2008000779
[E]—dc22   CIP
                                                       AC

Book Design by Lou Fancher
09 10 11 12 13 SCP 10 9 8 7 6 5 4 3 2
❖
First Edition

The King's Taster

by **Kenneth Oppel**

paintings by **Steve Johnson & Lou Fancher**

HarperCollins*Publishers*

My name's Max, and I eat like a king.

I'm the king's taster. I taste all his food before he eats it, to make sure it's not poisoned. I also get his leftovers, plus whatever anyone drops under the table.

I'm the king's taster, but I'm the cook's dog. We've been together since I was a pup.

He's the best cook in the kingdom. He lets me lick the bowls and eat the scraps.

Then, one day, we got a brand-new king.

The cook went straight to work on the coronation feast. He chopped, he topped, and he tailed; he sliced and he stirred and he whisked. He cooked wild boar, peacock, and venison. He baked cheese pies, rose puddings, and syllabub.

It was a feast
fit for a king!

I tasted the king's food.
It was delicious.

But the king only picked at his food until it was all mashed up.
"I will not eat this food," he said, and he pushed it to the floor.
No one said a word.
I ate the king's meal.

In the kitchen, the cook clutched at his hair.

"Why doesn't the new king like my food?" he cried.

I burped. I'd just eaten like a king.

"Max," the cook said, "this is a serious matter! Tomorrow night I've got to serve the king food he'll eat. But what?"

I barked.

"That's it!" the cook said. "I must get some new recipes! Not a second to lose!"

We harnessed the horses and left for France at once, and there, in the finest kitchens of Paris, we discovered a wondrous new concoction made from potatoes.

"The king will love this!" said the cook.

We made it home just before noon.

That night at dinner, the cook set the platter before the king and whisked off the top.

"Your Highness," he said, "may I offer you . . . French fries!"

I tasted the king's food. It was delicious.

But the king picked and poked at his food until it was mushy and all mashed up.

"I will not eat this food," the king said, and he lifted his plate and heaved it across the dining room.

No one said a word.

I ate the king's meal.

Back in the kitchen, the cook was banging
his head against the wall.

"This is terrible!" he cried.

I burped. After all, I'd just eaten like a king.

"Come on, Max, we've got another journey
ahead of us!"

We set sail for Italy at once. We glided by gondola through the canals of Venice, and in the Piazza San Marco, we learned of fabulous breads and herbs, sausages and cheeses.

"Our king won't be able to resist this!" said the cook.

We made it back home with only hours to spare.

"Your Highness," the cook said proudly, "from Italy
I bring you . . . pizza!"

I tasted the king's food. It was delicious.

But the king picked and poked and puffed at his food
until it was mushy and mucky and altogether mashed up.

"I will not eat this food," the King said.

And he put it in his catapult and fired it against the dining room wall.

No one said a word.

I ate the king's meal.

"This is no way to live, Max!" the cook said, tugging at his hair. "We'd better get it right this time."

We cast off our balloon at once and sailed through the skies across the great Atlantic. In Mexico, we journeyed by mule through thick green jungles,

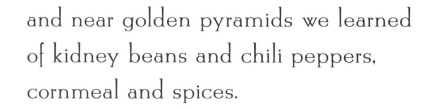

and near golden pyramids we learned of kidney beans and chili peppers, cornmeal and spices.

"This," the cook said, "will win the king over!"

We thanked our guides, soared up into the sky, and made it home with only minutes to spare.

"Chili tacos, Your Highness!" proclaimed the cook.
I tasted the king's food. It was stupendous!

But the king picked and poked
and puffed and plucked at his food
until it was mushy and muddy and
mucky and altogether mashed up.

Then he threw it out the window.
It landed with a plop in the moat.

"Off with his head!" the king
shouted at the cook, and stomped
away.

No one said a word.

My meal was eaten by crocodiles.

In the kitchen, the cook sat hunched over in his chair.

"That's it," he said sadly. "I'm finished, Max. The king's going to chop off my head."

He put away all his pots and pans, his whisks and knives and stirring spoons. He took off his apron and hung it on a peg.

"I wish I'd started my own place," said the cook. "I always wanted to. But maybe I'm just no good anymore."

"You're the best cook in the world," I barked, but I don't think he understood, so I licked his hand instead.

I couldn't sleep.
How could anyone not like the
cook's food? It didn't make sense.
I heard a cupboard door squeak.

I saw a shadow scuttling
out of the kitchen.
I followed.

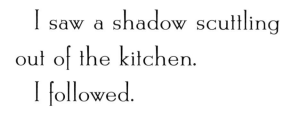

Outside the kitchen, there were crumbs
on the floor.
They tasted like almonds and sugar.
I followed the crumbs down the hall and
straight to the door of the king's bedroom!
I peeked through the keyhole.

I ran back to the cook's room and danced a jig on
his belly to wake him up.

Then I stood in the doorway and barked.

"All right, all right," he said, "I'm coming."

Outside the king's room, the cook peeked
through the keyhole.
"You're a good dog, Max," he whispered.
Then he opened the door without knocking.

"Hello, Your Highness!" he said.

The king was sitting in the middle of his enormous bed.

Eating candy.

The sheets were covered with liquorice allsorts and ginger cookies and huge hunks of marzipan, and he was gobbling like there was no tomorrow.

"How dare you enter my bedroom!" cried the king.

"Sire," said the cook, "I understand now why you don't eat my food. You've been filching candy from my kitchen, and you have spoiled your appetite! This must stop!"

"You can't tell me what to do!" he shouted. "I'm the king!"

"I will tell your mother," said the cook.

That stopped the king cold.

"You wouldn't," he said.

"I would," said the cook. "And I will."

The next night at dinner, the king tried his food.
The night after, he tried a little more.
And the night after that, he ate everything on his plate.

"Cook!" he cried. "Your food is fit for a king!"

"And you, Your Highness," the cook replied, "are at last eating like a king."

"Ask me for anything," the king said, "and it shall be yours!"

I'm not the king's taster anymore.
But I'm still the cook's dog. And
he's the best cook in the world.
We've got our own place now.
Where everyone eats like a king.